A DAY WITH A VETERINARIAN

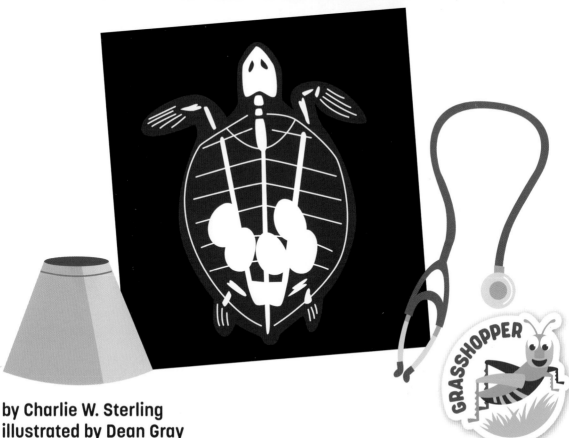

by Charlie W. Sterling
illustrated by Dean Gray

Tools for Parents & Teachers

Grasshopper Books enhance imagination and introduce the earliest readers to fiction with fun storylines and illustrations. The easy-to-read text supports early reading experiences with repetitive sentence patterns and sight words.

Before Reading

- Discuss the cover illustration. What do they see?

- Look at the picture glossary together. Discuss the words.

Read the Book

- Read the book to the child, or have him or her read independently.

- "Walk" through the book and look at the illustrations. Who is the main character? What is happening in the story?

After Reading

- Prompt the child to think more. Ask: Would you like to be a veterinarian? Why or why not?

Grasshopper Books are published by Jump!
5357 Penn Avenue South
Minneapolis, MN 55419
www.jumplibrary.com

Library of Congress Cataloging-in-Publication Data

Names: Sterling, Charlie W., author. | Gray, Dean, illustrator.
Title: A day with a veterinarian / by Charlie W. Sterling; illustrated by Dean Gray.
Description: Minneapolis, MN: Jump!, Inc., 2022.
Series: Meet the community helpers!
Includes index.
Audience: Ages 5-8.
Identifiers: LCCN 2021034101 (print)
LCCN 2021034102 (ebook)
ISBN 9781636903316 (hardcover)
ISBN 9781636903323 (paperback)
ISBN 9781636903330 (ebook)
Subjects: LCSH: Readers (Primary)
Veterinarians–Juvenile fiction.
LCGFT: Readers (Publications)
Classification: LCC P
DDC 428.6/2–dc23
LC record available at https://lccn.loc.gov/2021034101
LC ebook record available at https://lccn.loc.gov/2021034102

Editor: Eliza Leahy
Direction and Layout: Anna Peterson
Illustrator: Dean Gray

Printed in the United States of America at Corporate Graphics in North Mankato, Minnesota.

Table of Contents

Caring for Pets 4

Quiz Time! 22

Veterinarian Tools 22

Picture Glossary 23

Index 24

To Learn More 24

Caring for Pets

It is a busy day at the veterinarian's office.

Dr. Jenny has a lot of pets to see!

Dr. Jenny gives Rex an exam.

She checks his ears and eyes.

She checks his nose, tail, and paws, too.

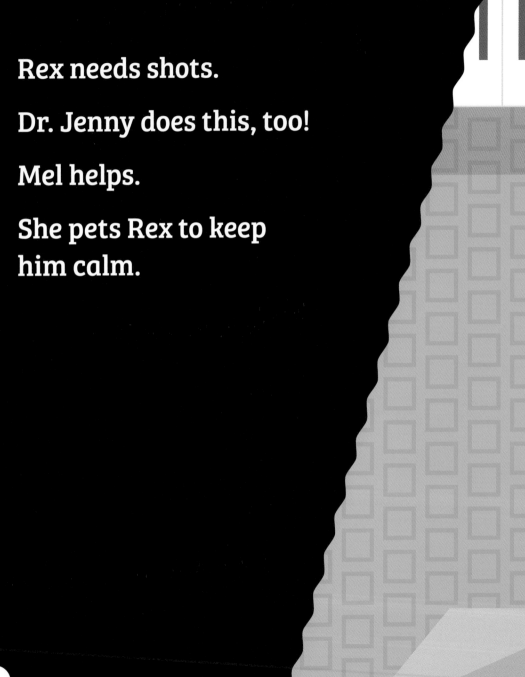

Rex needs shots.

Dr. Jenny does this, too!

Mel helps.

She pets Rex to keep him calm.

Hopper's appointment
is next.

He gets his teeth checked.

"Looking good!"
Dr. Jenny says.

11

Polly is next.

Dr. Jenny trims her beak.

Why?

12

It could grow too long.

"Pretty bird!" says Dr. Jenny.

Tia the turtle is going
to have babies!

Dr. Jenny takes an X-ray.

It shows the eggs inside!

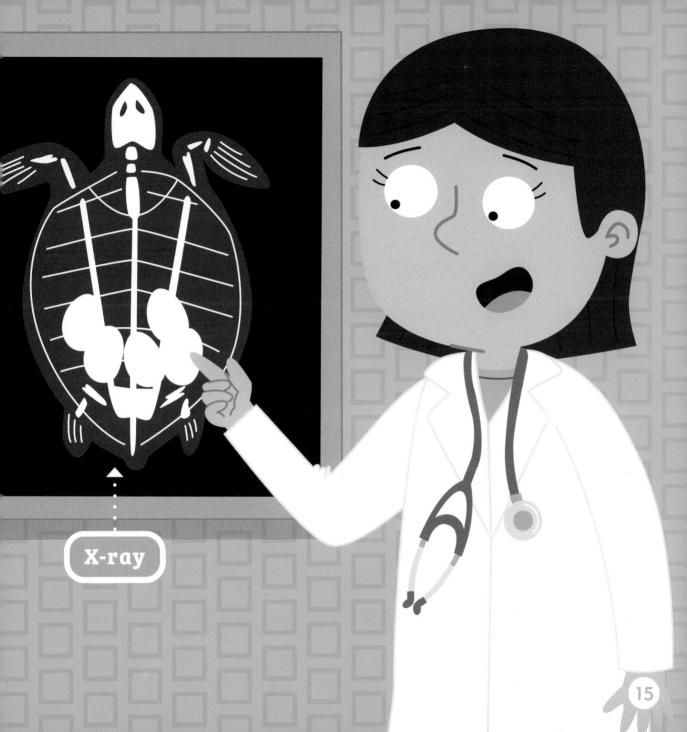

X-ray

Sox got something stuck in her paw.

Dr. Jenny gets it out.

Then she cleans and bandages Sox's paw.

bandage

She puts a cone on Sox.

"Why does she need a cone?" asks Sam.

"That way she can't lick her paw.
It will heal faster," says Dr. Jenny.

Dr. Jenny hands them
Sox's medication.

"Thanks, Dr. Jenny!"
says Sam.

"You're welcome," says Dr. Jenny. "See you in a few weeks for Sox's next exam!"

Quiz Time!

What pet didn't Dr. Jenny see and treat today?

A. dog **B.** cat **C.** fish **D.** turtle

Veterinarian Tools

Take a look at some of a veterinarian's tools!

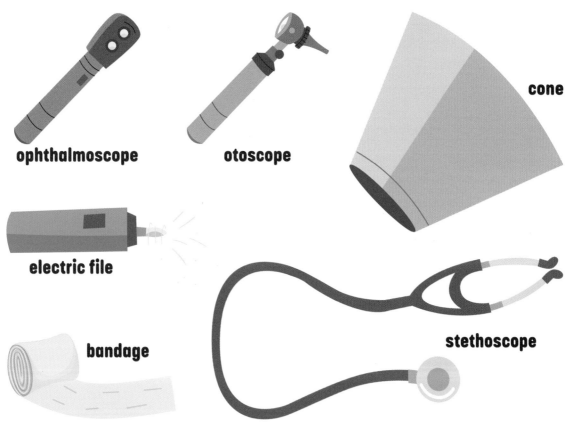

ophthalmoscope

otoscope

cone

electric file

bandage

stethoscope

Quiz Time! Answer Key: **C.** fish

Picture Glossary

appointment
An arrangement to meet someone at a certain time.

bandages
Puts on a piece of material that protects an injured body part while it heals.

exam
A careful check a veterinarian does of an animal's body.

medication
A substance used to treat an injury or illness.

veterinarian
A doctor who is trained to diagnose and treat sick or injured animals.

X-ray
A picture of the inside of one's body.

Index

appointment 5, 10

babies 14

bandages 16

beak 12

checks 6, 10

cleans 16

cone 17

eggs 14

exam 6, 20

heal 17

medication 18

paws 6, 16, 17

pets 8

shots 8

teeth 10

trims 12

veterinarian's office 4

X-ray 14

To Learn More

Finding more information is as easy as 1, 2, 3.

❶ Go to www.factsurfer.com

❷ Enter "**adaywithaveterinarian**" into the search box.

❸ Choose your book to see a list of websites.

FACT SURFER